D0506809

MY LITTLE PONY

FRIENDS FOREVER

PINKIE PIE & APPLEJACK

Written and Lettered by
Alex De Campi

Art by
Carla Speed McNeil

Colored by
Jenn Manley Lee and **Bill Mudron**

 Spotlight

ABDOPUBLISHING.COM

Reinforced library bound edition published in 2017 by Spotlight,
a division of ABDO, PO Box 398166, Minneapolis, Minnesota 55439.
Spotlight produces high-quality reinforced library bound editions for
schools and libraries. Published by agreement with IDW.

Printed in the United States of America, North Mankato, Minnesota.
042016
092016

THIS BOOK CONTAINS
RECYCLED MATERIALS

Licensed By:

LIBRARY OF CONGRESS CATALOGING-IN-PUBLICATION DATA

Names: De Campi, Alex, author. | McNeil, Carla Speed, illustrator.
Title: Pinkie Pie & Applejack / writer, Alex De Campi ; art, Carla Speed
   McNeil ; colors, Jenn Manley Lee and Bill Mudron.
Description: Reinforced library bound edition. | Minneapolis, Minnesota :
   Spotlight, 2017. | Series: My little pony: friends forever
Identifiers: LCCN 2016000298 | ISBN 9781614795087
Subjects: LCSH: Graphic novels.
Classification: LCC PZ7.7.D43 Pi 2016 | DDC 741.5/973--dc23
LC record available at https://lccn.loc.gov/2016000298

Spotlight

A Division of ABDO
abdopublishing.com

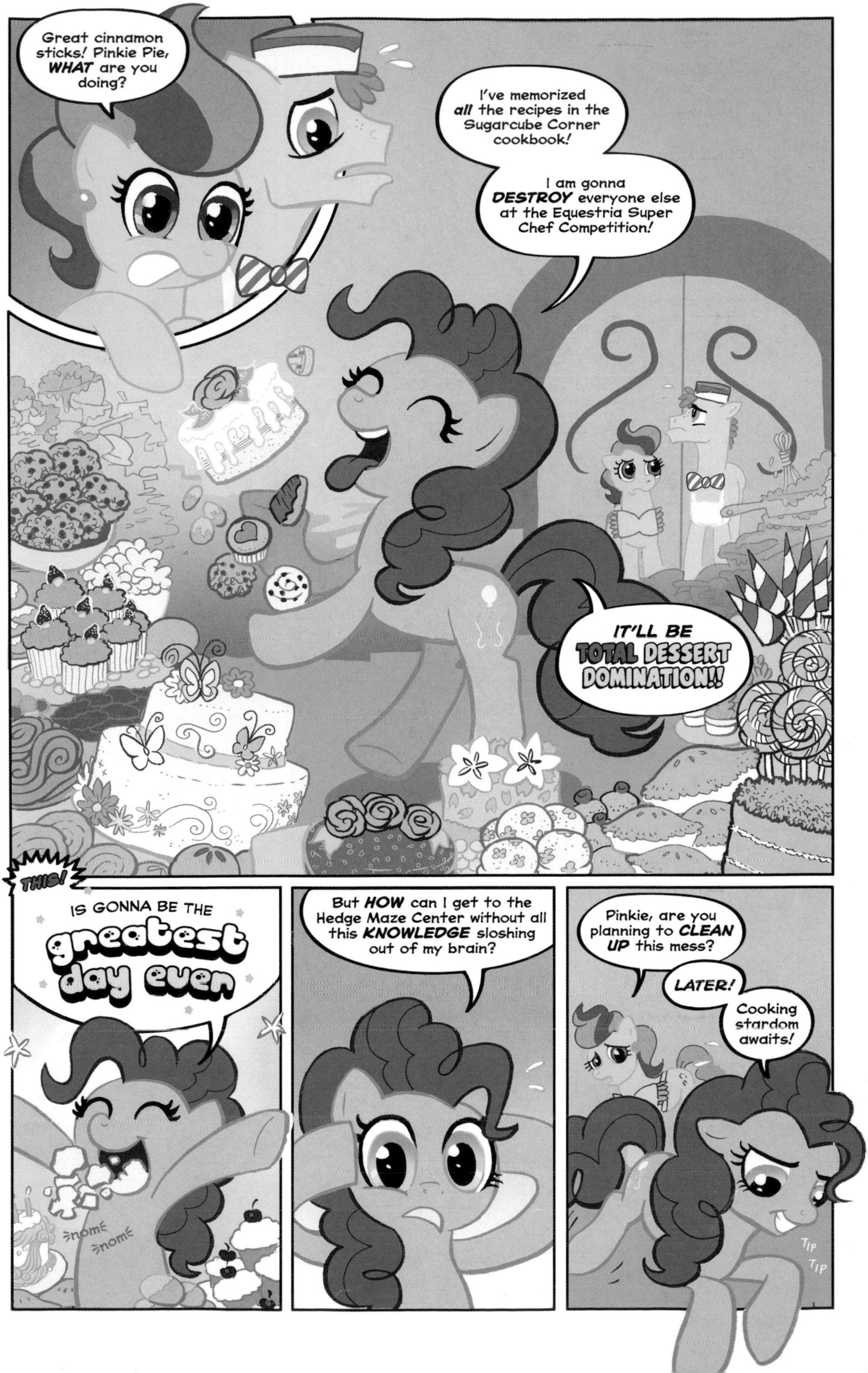
Great cinnamon sticks! Pinkie Pie, WHAT are you doing?
I've memorized all the recipes in the Sugarcube Corner cookbook!
I am gonna DESTROY everyone else at the Equestria Super Chef Competition!
IT'LL BE TOTAL DESSERT DOMINATION!!
THIS!
IS GONNA BE THE greatest day ever
nom nom
But HOW can I get to the Hedge Maze Center without all this KNOWLEDGE sloshing out of my brain?
Pinkie, are you planning to CLEAN UP this mess?
LATER!
Cooking stardom awaits!
TIP TIP

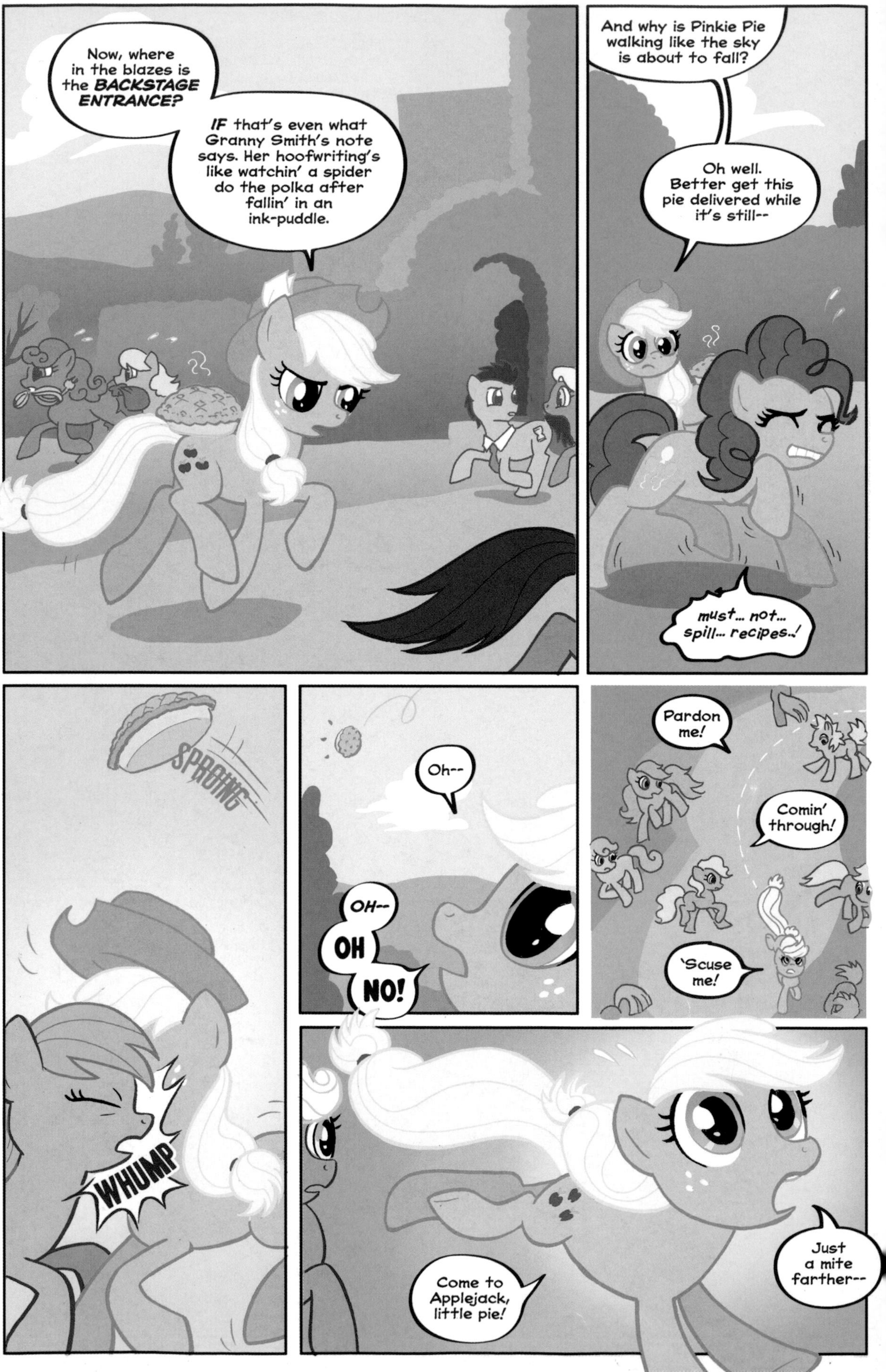
Now, where in the blazes is the BACKSTAGE ENTRANCE?
IF that's even what Granny Smith's note says. Her hoofwriting's like watchin' a spider do the polka after fallin' in an ink-puddle.
And why is Pinkie Pie walking like the sky is about to fall?
Oh well. Better get this pie delivered while it's still--
must... not... spill... recipes..!
SPROING
WHUMP
Oh--
OH--
OH
NO!
Pardon me!
Comin' through!
'Scuse me!
Come to Applejack, little pie!
Just a mite farther--

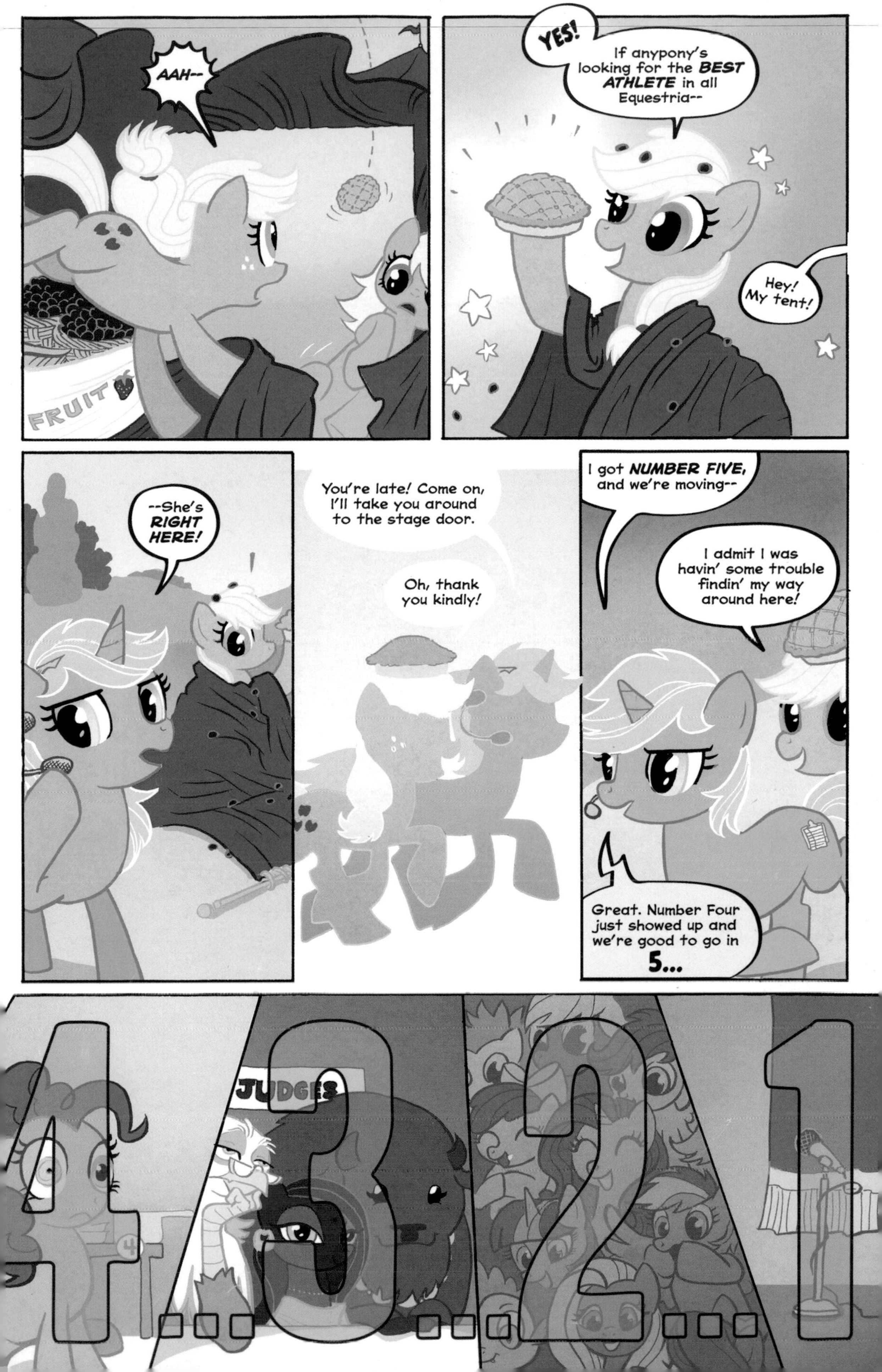
AAH--
YES!
If anypony's looking for the BEST ATHLETE in all Equestria--
Hey! My tent!
FRUIT
--She's RIGHT HERE!
You're late! Come on, I'll take you around to the stage door.
Oh, thank you kindly!
I got NUMBER FIVE, and we're moving--
I admit I was havin' some trouble findin' my way around here!
Great. Number Four just showed up and we're good to go in
5...
4...
JUDGES
3...
2...
1

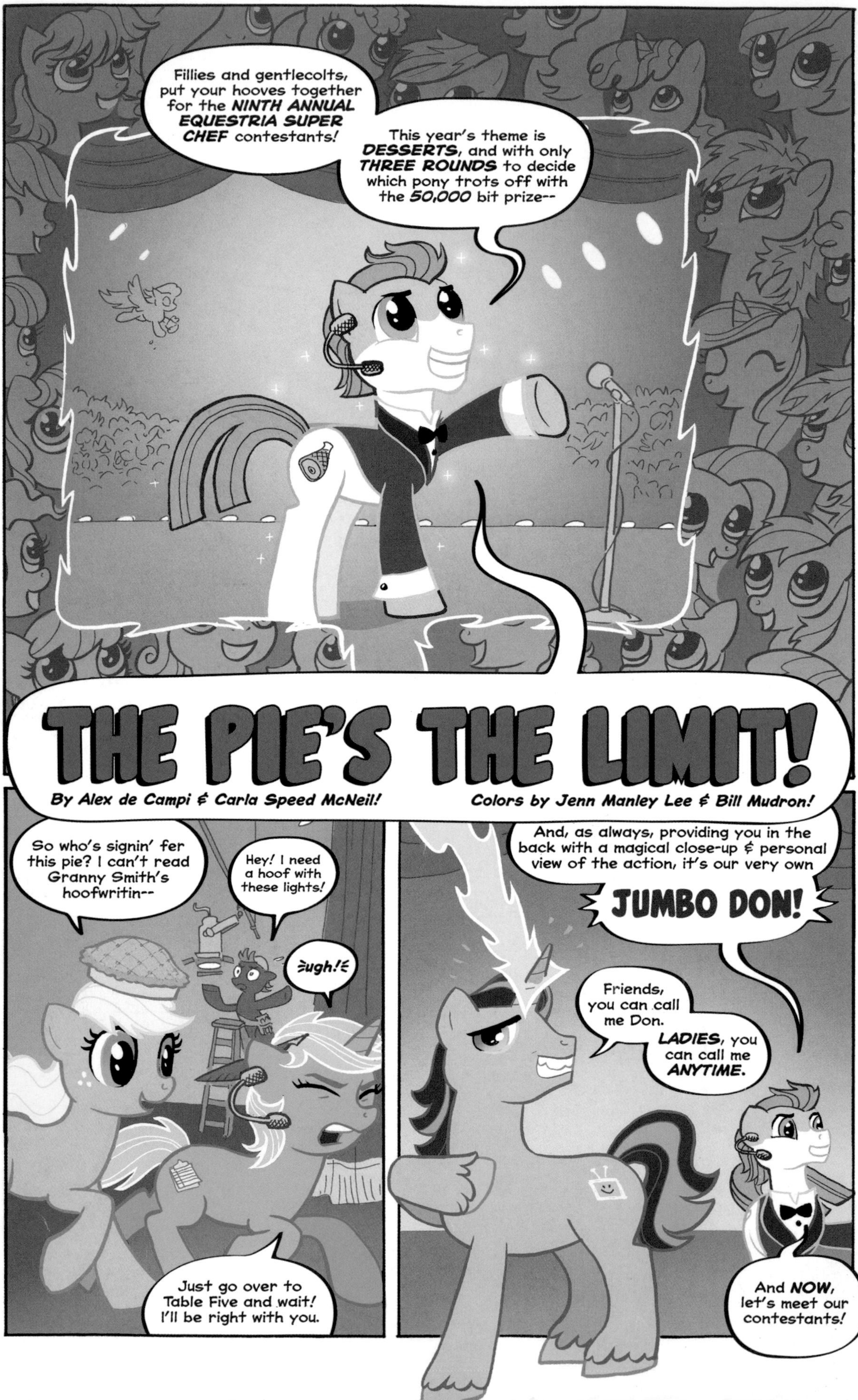
Fillies and gentlecolts, put your hooves together for the NINTH ANNUAL EQUESTRIA SUPER CHEF contestants!
This year's theme is DESSERTS, and with only THREE ROUNDS to decide which pony trots off with the 50,000 bit prize--
THE PIE'S THE LIMIT!
By Alex de Campi & Carla Speed McNeil!
Colors by Jenn Manley Lee & Bill Mudron!
So who's signin' fer this pie? I can't read Granny Smith's hoofwritin--
Hey! I need a hoof with these lights!
ugh!
Just go over to Table Five and wait! I'll be right with you.
And, as always, providing you in the back with a magical close-up & personal view of the action, it's our very own
JUMBO DON!
Friends, you can call me Don.
LADIES, you can call me ANYTIME.
And NOW, let's meet our contestants!

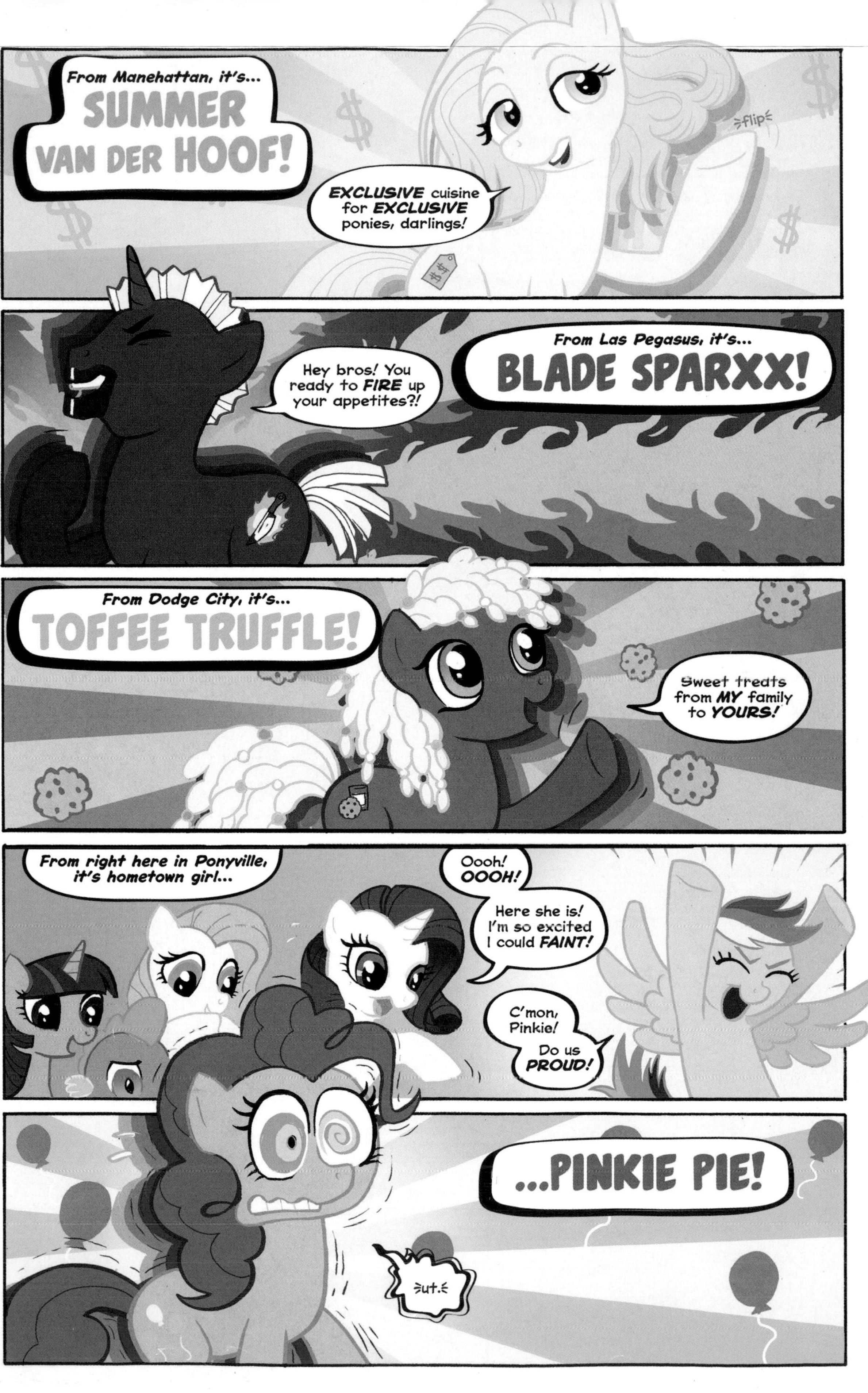

From Manehattan, it's...
SUMMER VAN DER HOOF!
flip
EXCLUSIVE cuisine for EXCLUSIVE ponies, darlings!
Hey bros! You ready to FIRE up your appetites?!
From Las Pegasus, it's...
BLADE SPARXX!
From Dodge City, it's...
TOFFEE TRUFFLE!
Sweet treats from MY family to YOURS!
From right here in Ponyville, it's hometown girl...
Oooh! OOOH!
Here she is! I'm so excited I could FAINT!
C'mon, Pinkie!
Do us PROUD!
...PINKIE PIE!
ut.

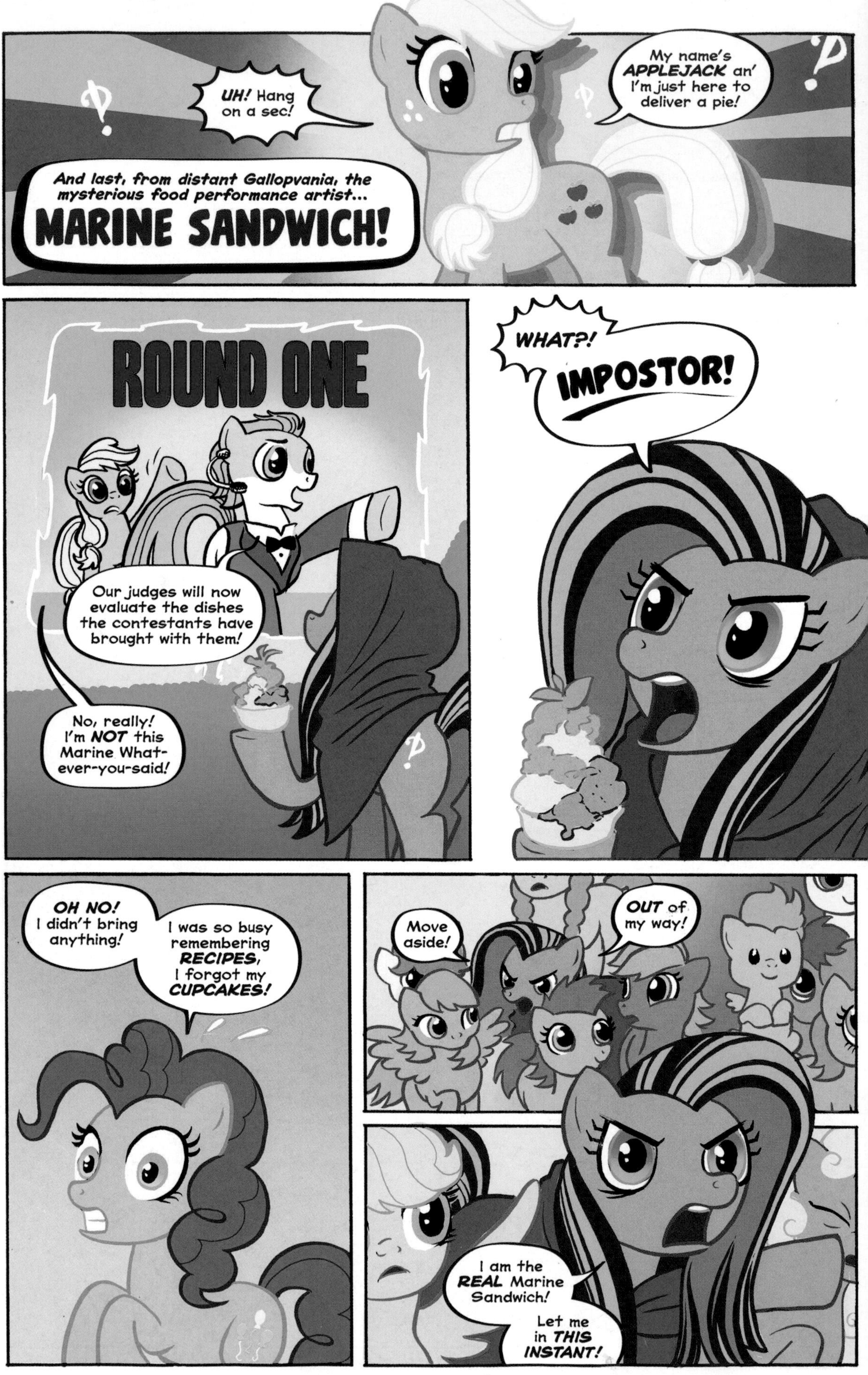
And last, from distant Gallopvania, the mysterious food performance artist...
MARINE SANDWICH!
UH! Hang on a sec!
My name's APPLEJACK an' I'm just here to deliver a pie!
ROUND ONE
Our judges will now evaluate the dishes the contestants have brought with them!
No, really! I'm NOT this Marine What-ever-you-said!
WHAT?!
IMPOSTOR!
OH NO! I didn't bring anything!
I was so busy remembering RECIPES, I forgot my CUPCAKES!
Move aside!
OUT of my way!
I am the REAL Marine Sandwich!
Let me in THIS INSTANT!

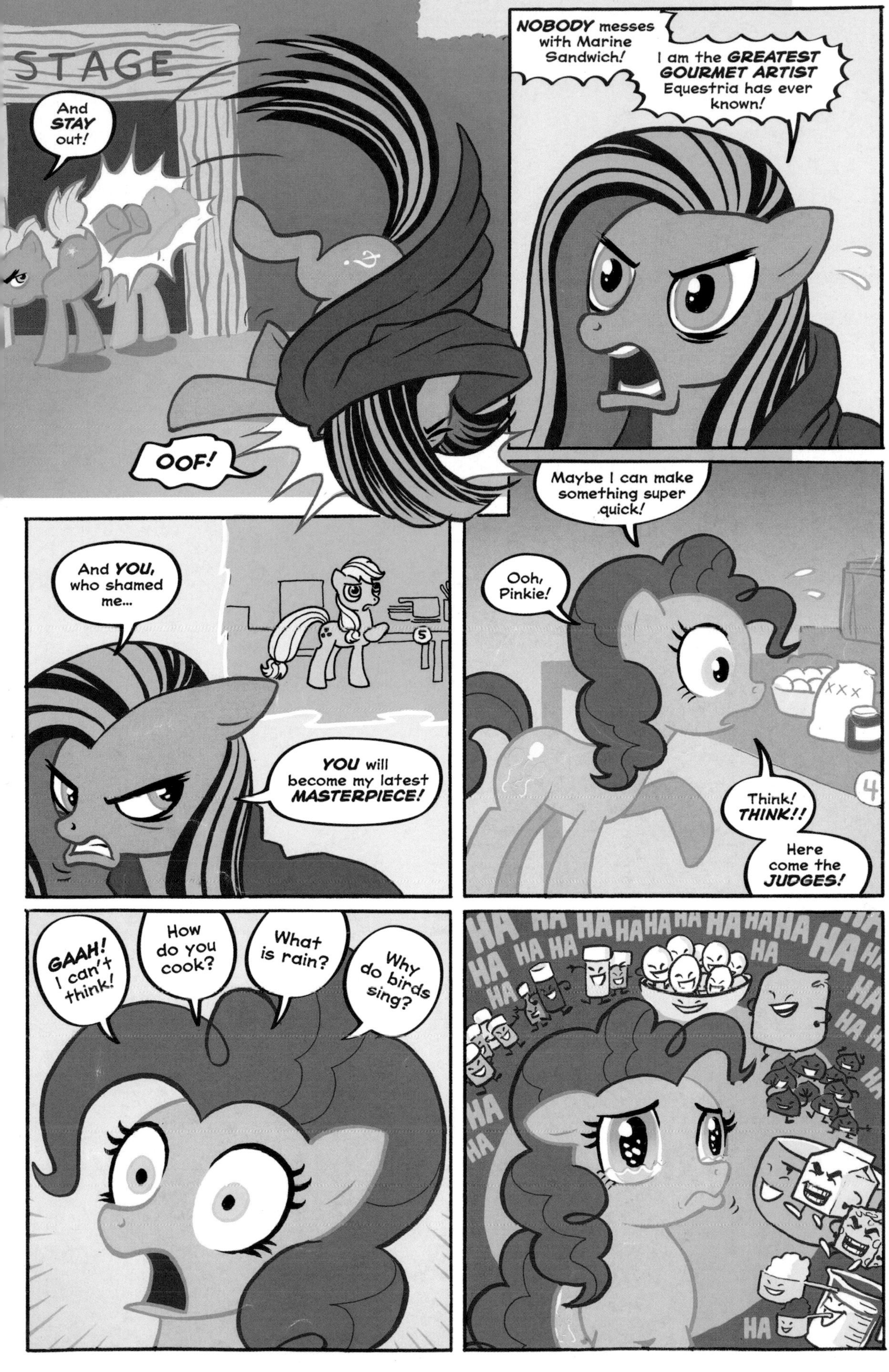
STAGE
And STAY out!
OOF!
NOBODY messes with Marine Sandwich!
I am the GREATEST GOURMET ARTIST Equestria has ever known!
And YOU, who shamed me...
YOU will become my latest MASTERPIECE!
Maybe I can make something super quick!
Ooh, Pinkie!
Think! THINK!!
Here come the JUDGES!
GAAH! I can't think!
How do you cook?
What is rain?
Why do birds sing?
HA HA HA HA HA HA HA HA HA HA HA HA

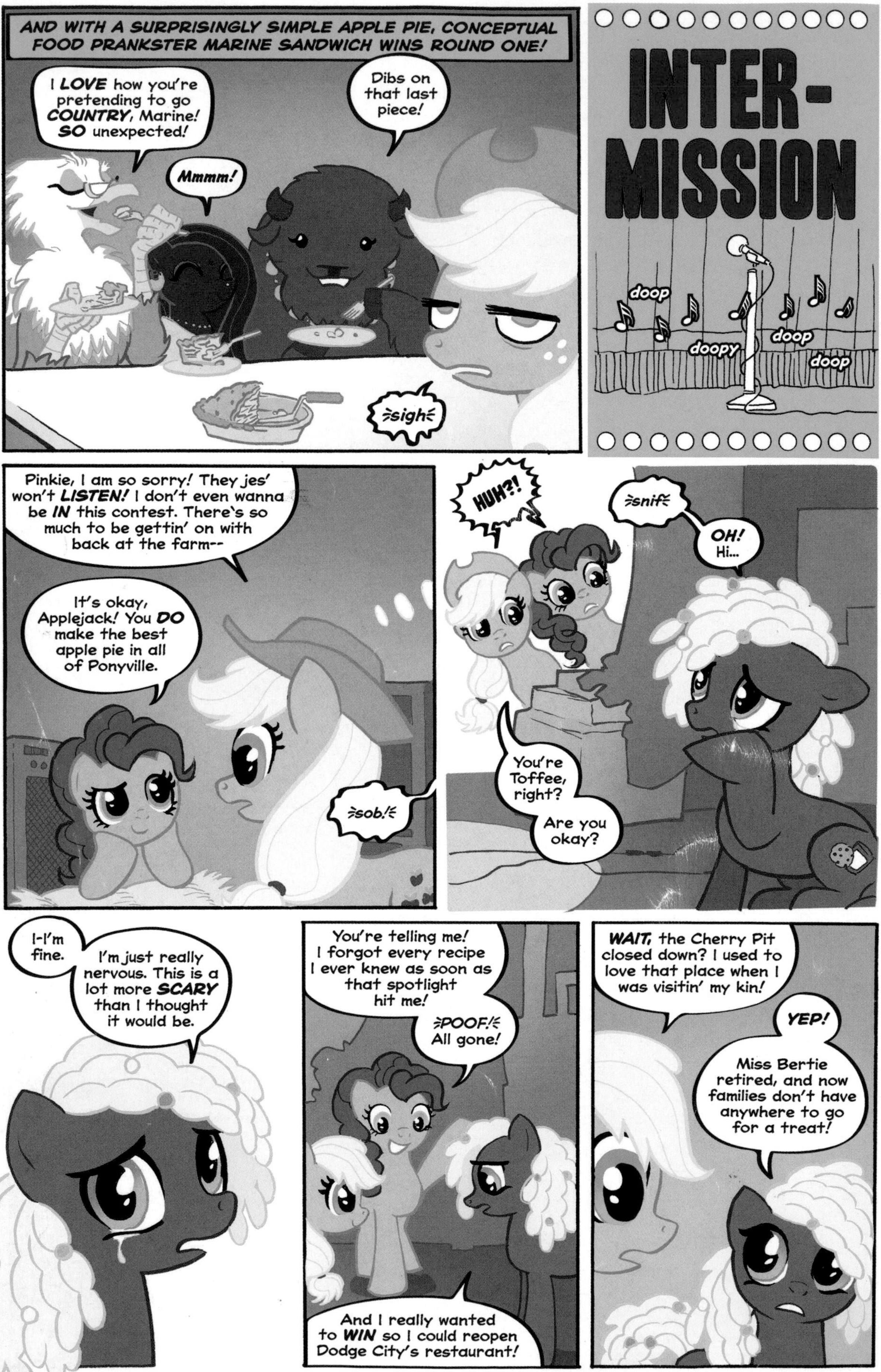
AND WITH A SURPRISINGLY SIMPLE APPLE PIE, CONCEPTUAL FOOD PRANKSTER MARINE SANDWICH WINS ROUND ONE!
I LOVE how you're pretending to go COUNTRY, Marine! SO unexpected!
Mmmm!
Dibs on that last piece!
sigh
INTER-MISSION
doop
doopy
doop
doop
Pinkie, I am so sorry! They jes' won't LISTEN! I don't even wanna be IN this contest. There's so much to be gettin' on with back at the farm--
It's okay, Applejack! You DO make the best apple pie in all of Ponyville.
sob!
HUH?!
snif
OH! Hi...
You're Toffee, right?
Are you okay?
I-I'm fine.
I'm just really nervous. This is a lot more SCARY than I thought it would be.
You're telling me! I forgot every recipe I ever knew as soon as that spotlight hit me!
POOF! All gone!
And I really wanted to WIN so I could reopen Dodge City's restaurant!
WAIT, the Cherry Pit closed down? I used to love that place when I was visitin' my kin!
YEP!
Miss Bertie retired, and now families don't have anywhere to go for a treat!

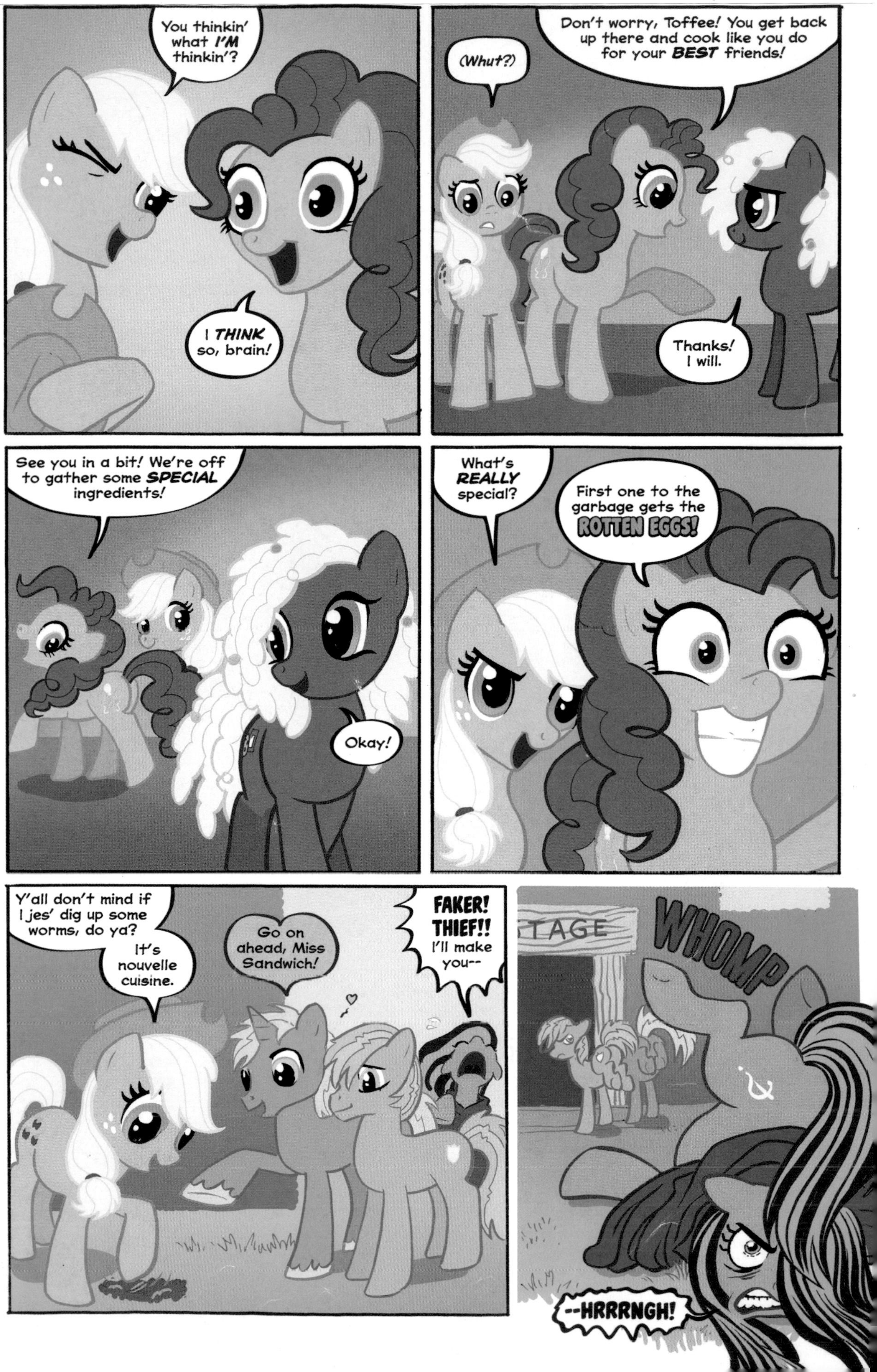

You thinkin' what I'M thinkin'?
I THINK so, brain!
(Whut?)
Don't worry, Toffee! You get back up there and cook like you do for your BEST friends!
Thanks! I will.
See you in a bit! We're off to gather some SPECIAL ingredients!
Okay!
What's REALLY special?
First one to the garbage gets the ROTTEN EGGS!
Y'all don't mind if I jes' dig up some worms, do ya?
It's nouvelle cuisine.
Go on ahead, Miss Sandwich!
FAKER! THIEF!! I'll make you--
STAGE
WHOMP
--HRRRNGH!

ROUND TWO

Something with *CHOCOLATE!*

>skritch< >skrib<
>skribble<
>skrib<

SNIFF

CLAT CLAT

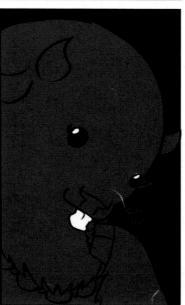

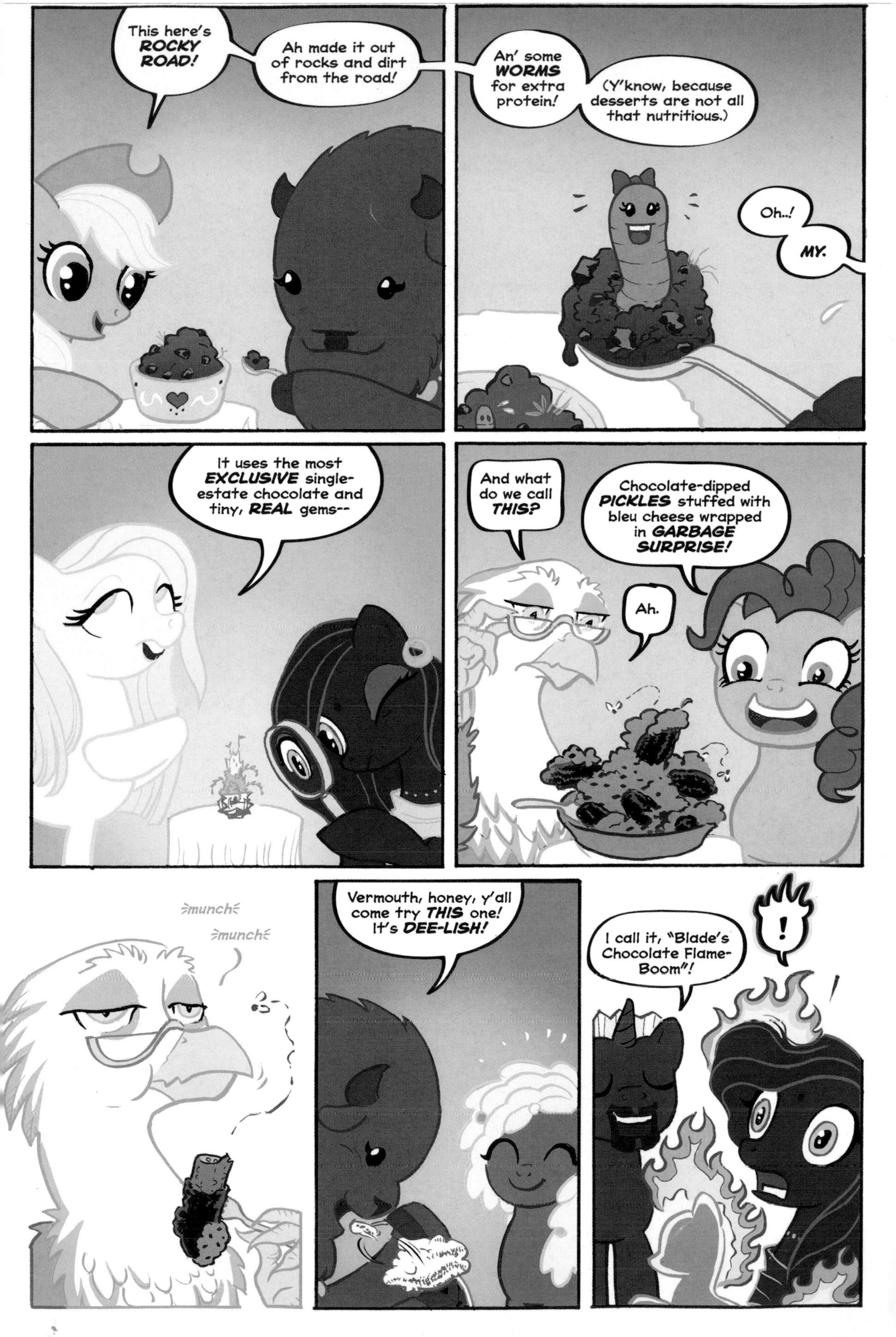

This here's ROCKY ROAD!
Ah made it out of rocks and dirt from the road!
An' some WORMS for extra protein!
(Y'know, because desserts are not all that nutritious.)
Oh..!
MY.
It uses the most EXCLUSIVE single-estate chocolate and tiny, REAL gems--
And what do we call THIS?
Chocolate-dipped PICKLES stuffed with bleu cheese wrapped in GARBAGE SURPRISE!
Ah.
munch
munch
Vermouth, honey, y'all come try THIS one! It's DEE-LISH!
I call it, "Blade's Chocolate Flame-Boom"!
!

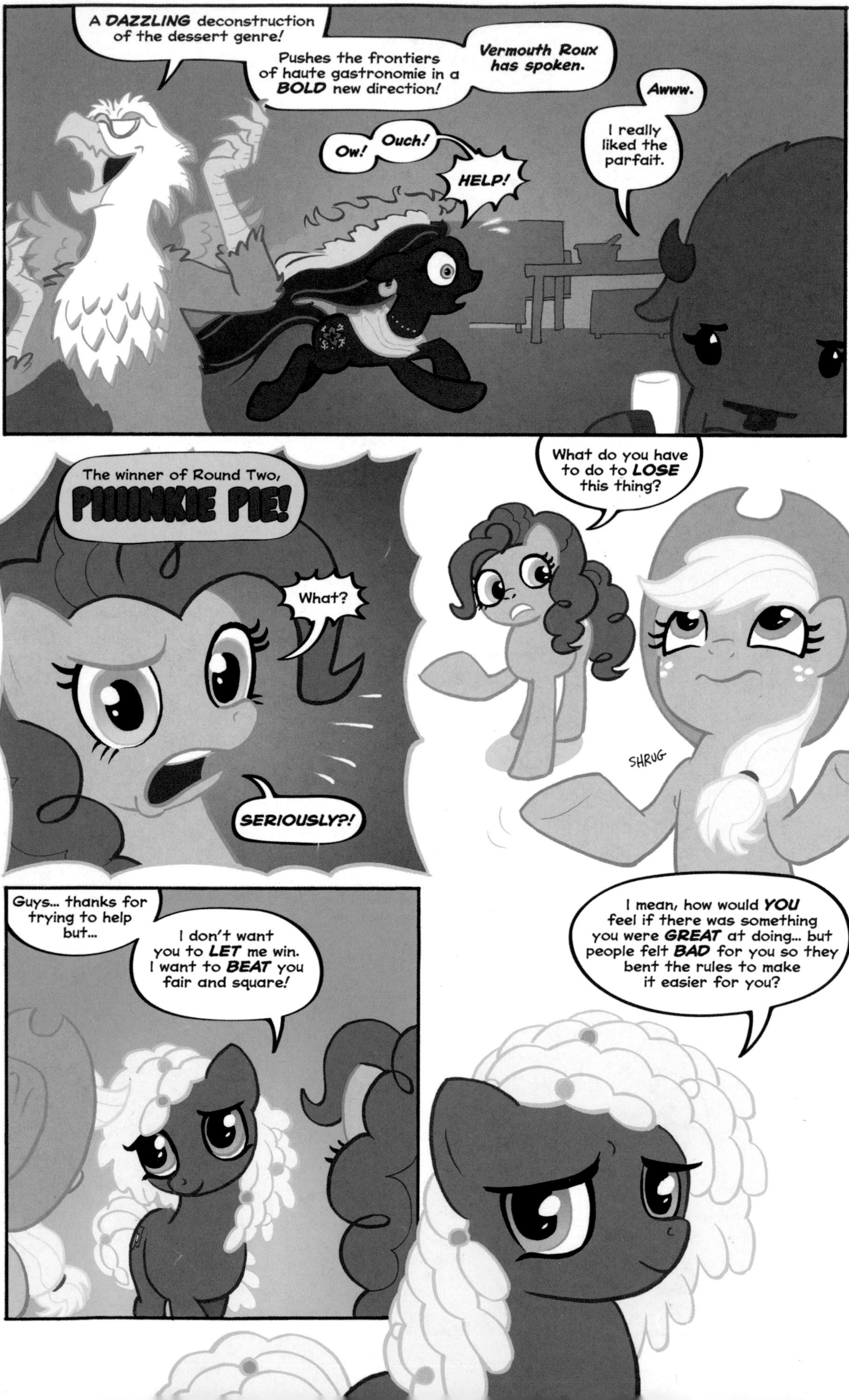

A DAZZLING deconstruction of the dessert genre!
Pushes the frontiers of haute gastronomie in a BOLD new direction!
Vermouth Roux has spoken.
Ow!
Ouch!
HELP!
Awww.
I really liked the parfait.
The winner of Round Two, PIIIINKIE PIE!
What?
SERIOUSLY?!
What do you have to do to LOSE this thing?
SHRUG
Guys... thanks for trying to help but...
I don't want you to LET me win. I want to BEAT you fair and square!
I mean, how would YOU feel if there was something you were GREAT at doing... but people felt BAD for you so they bent the rules to make it easier for you?

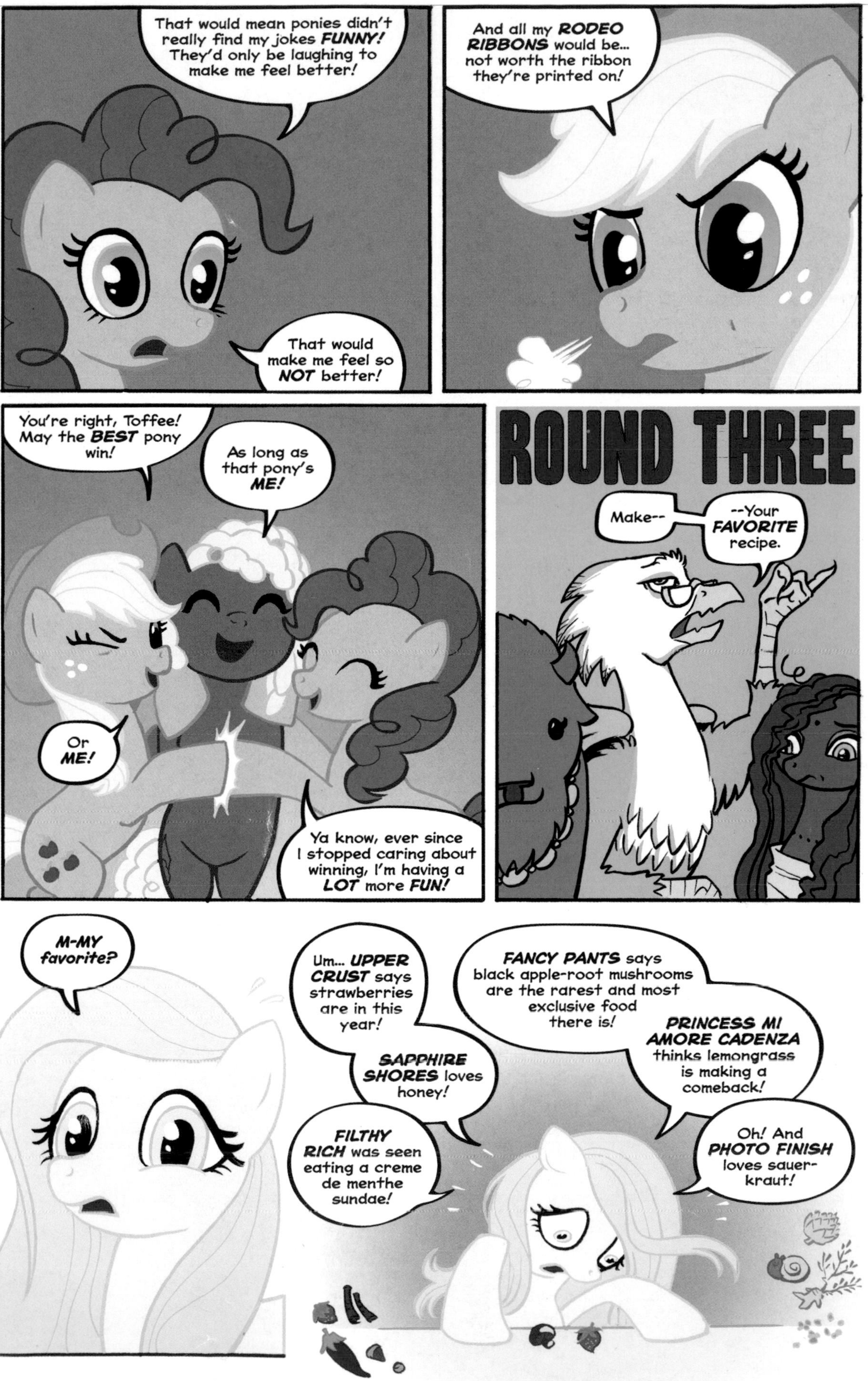

That would mean ponies didn't really find my jokes FUNNY! They'd only be laughing to make me feel better!
That would make me feel so NOT better!
And all my RODEO RIBBONS would be... not worth the ribbon they're printed on!
You're right, Toffee! May the BEST pony win!
As long as that pony's ME!
Or ME!
Ya know, ever since I stopped caring about winning, I'm having a LOT more FUN!
ROUND THREE
Make--
--Your FAVORITE recipe.
M-MY favorite?
Um... UPPER CRUST says strawberries are in this year!
SAPPHIRE SHORES loves honey!
FILTHY RICH was seen eating a creme de menthe sundae!
FANCY PANTS says black apple-root mushrooms are the rarest and most exclusive food there is!
PRINCESS MI AMORE CADENZA thinks lemongrass is making a comeback!
Oh! And PHOTO FINISH loves sauer-kraut!

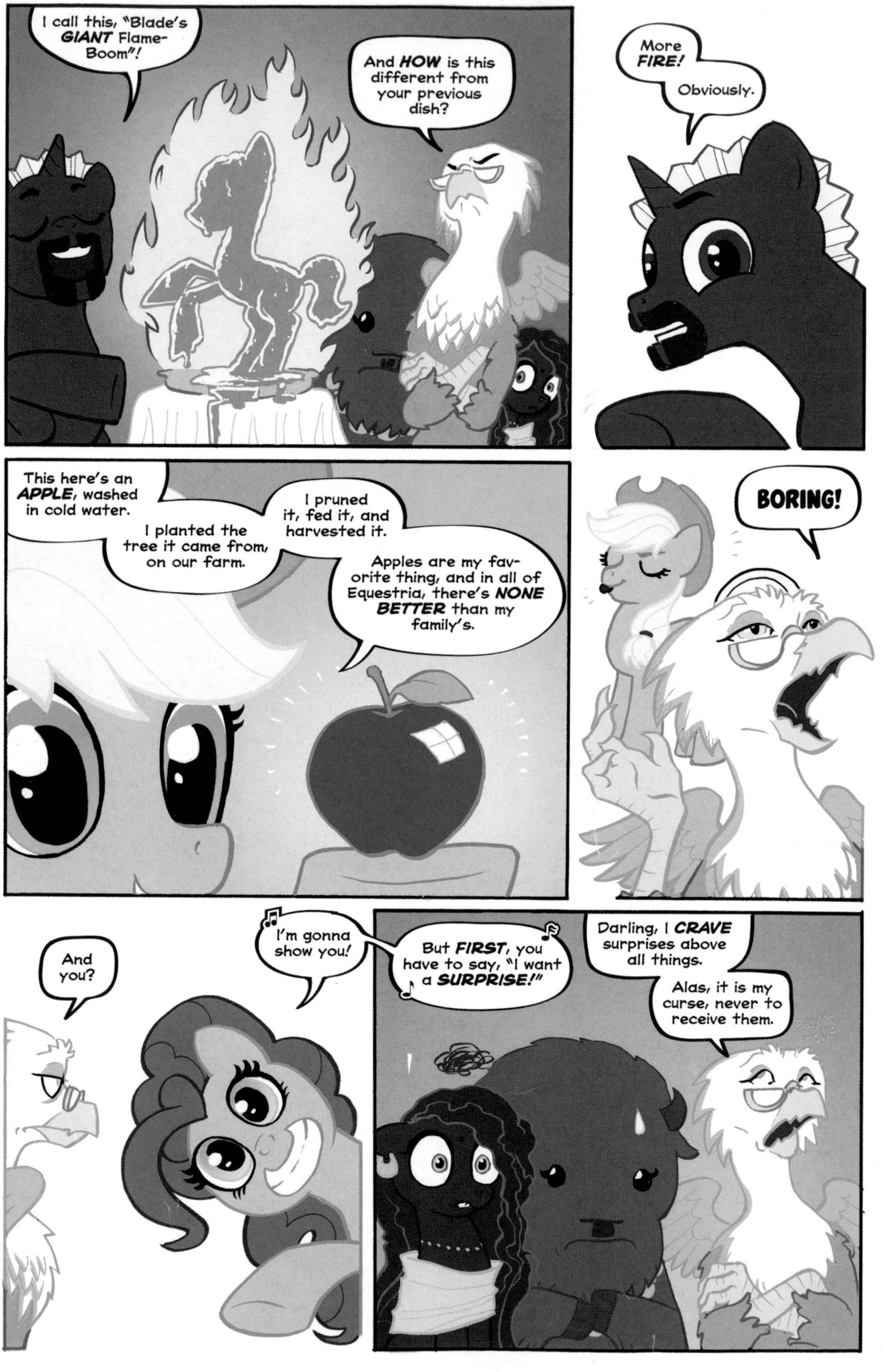
I call this, "Blade's GIANT Flame-Boom"!
And HOW is this different from your previous dish?
More FIRE!
Obviously.
This here's an APPLE, washed in cold water.
I planted the tree it came from, on our farm.
I pruned it, fed it, and harvested it.
Apples are my fav-orite thing, and in all of Equestria, there's NONE BETTER than my family's.
BORING!
And you?
I'm gonna show you!
But FIRST, you have to say, "I want a SURPRISE!"
Darling, I CRAVE surprises above all things.
Alas, it is my curse, never to receive them.

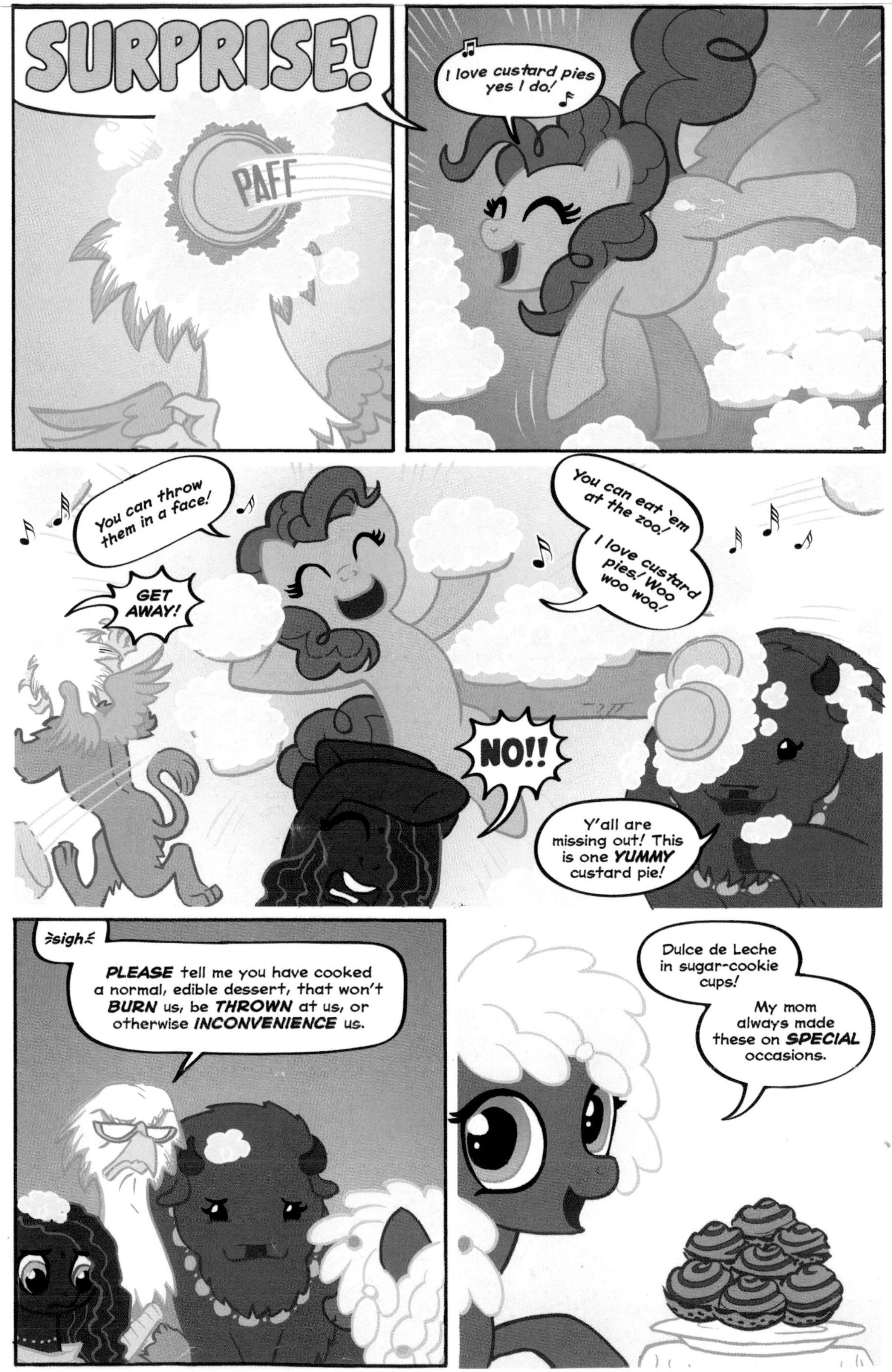
SURPRISE!
PAFF
I love custard pies yes I do!
You can throw them in a face!
GET AWAY!
You can eat 'em at the zoo!
I love custard pies! Woo woo woo!
NO!!
Y'all are missing out! This is one YUMMY custard pie!
sigh
PLEASE tell me you have cooked a normal, edible dessert, that won't BURN us, be THROWN at us, or otherwise INCONVENIENCE us.
Dulce de Leche in sugar-cookie cups!
My mom always made these on SPECIAL occasions.

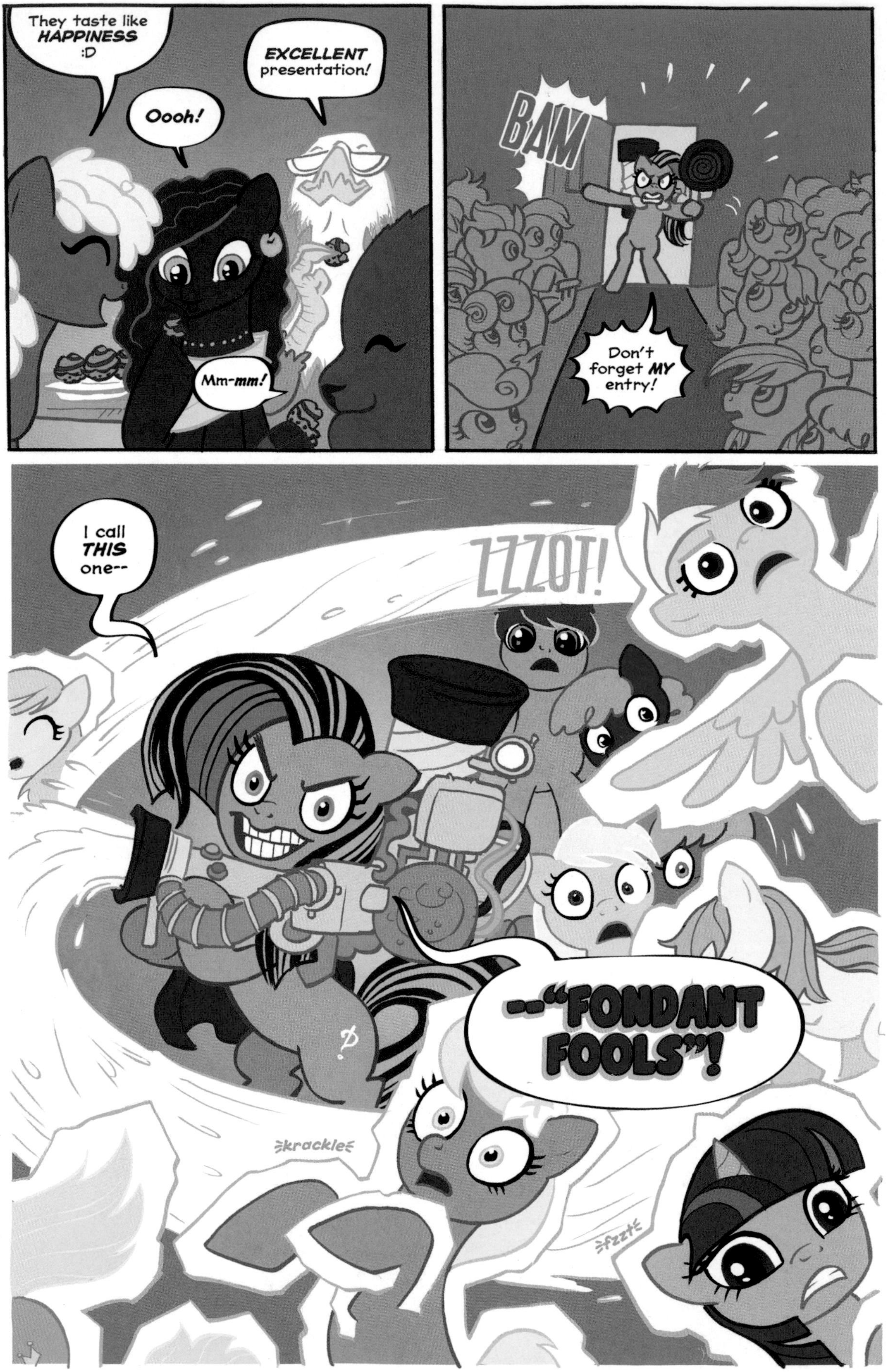

They taste like HAPPINESS :D
Oooh!
EXCELLENT presentation!
Mm-mm!
BAM
Don't forget MY entry!
I call THIS one--
ZZZOT!
--"FONDANT FOOLS"!
krackle
fzzt

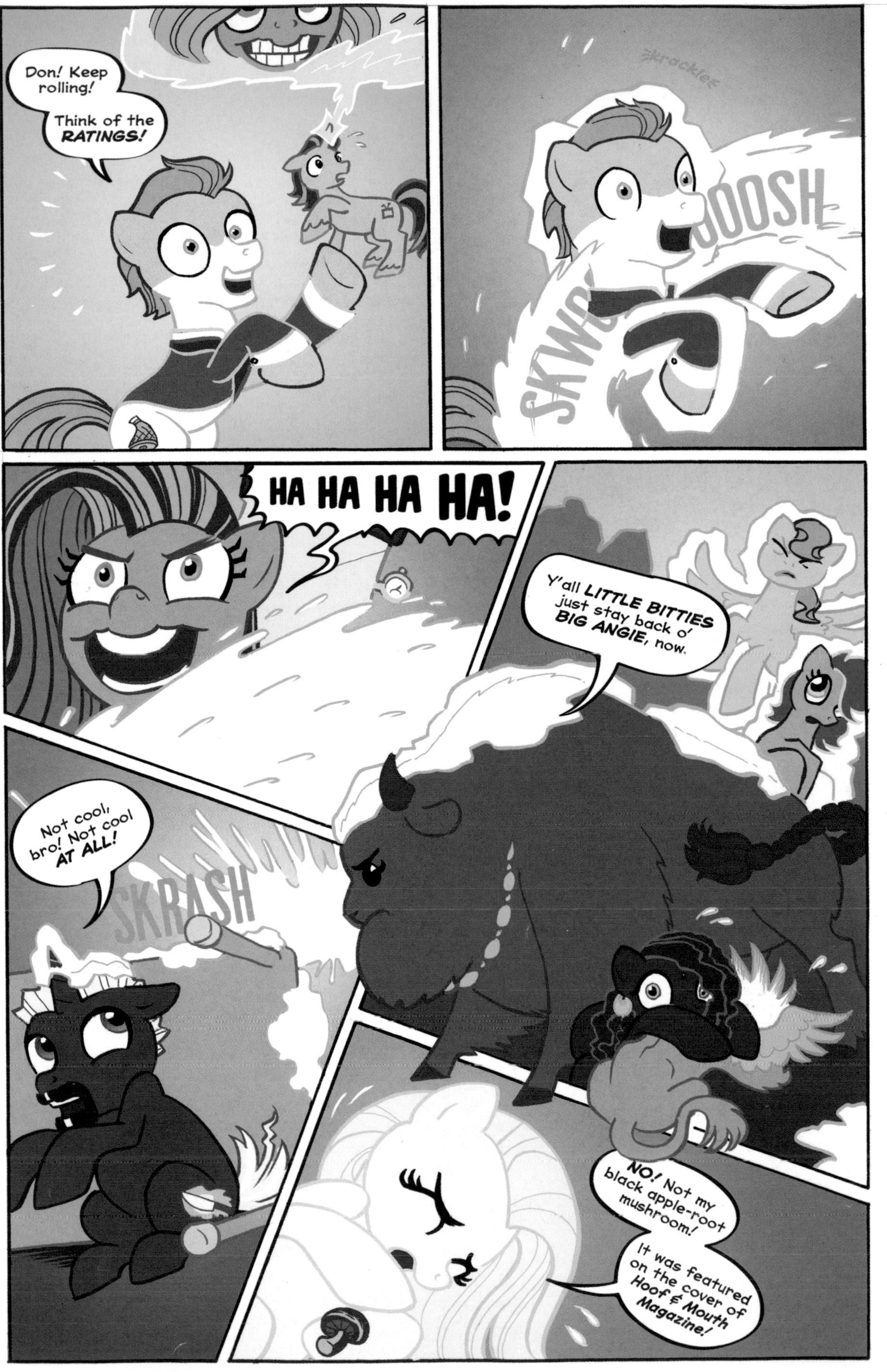

Don! Keep rolling!
Think of the RATINGS!
skrackle
SKWOOSH
HA HA HA HA!
Y'all LITTLE BITTIES just stay back o' BIG ANGIE, now.
Not cool, bro! Not cool AT ALL!
SKRASH
NO! Not my black apple-root mushroom!
It was featured on the cover of Hoof & Mouth Magazine!

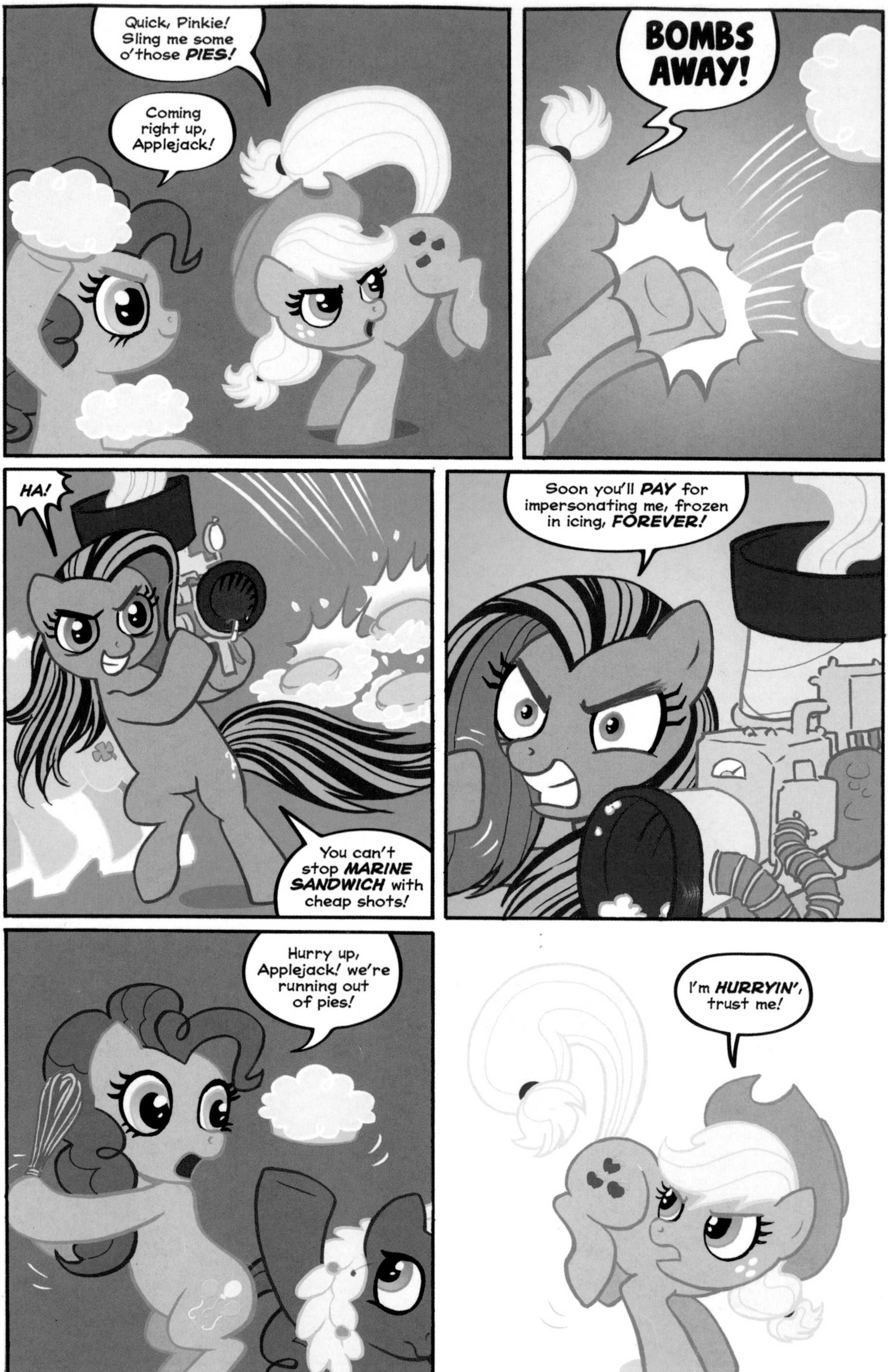
Quick, Pinkie! Sling me some o'those PIES!
Coming right up, Applejack!
BOMBS AWAY!
HA!
You can't stop MARINE SANDWICH with cheap shots!
Soon you'll PAY for impersonating me, frozen in icing, FOREVER!
Hurry up, Applejack! we're running out of pies!
I'm HURRYIN', trust me!

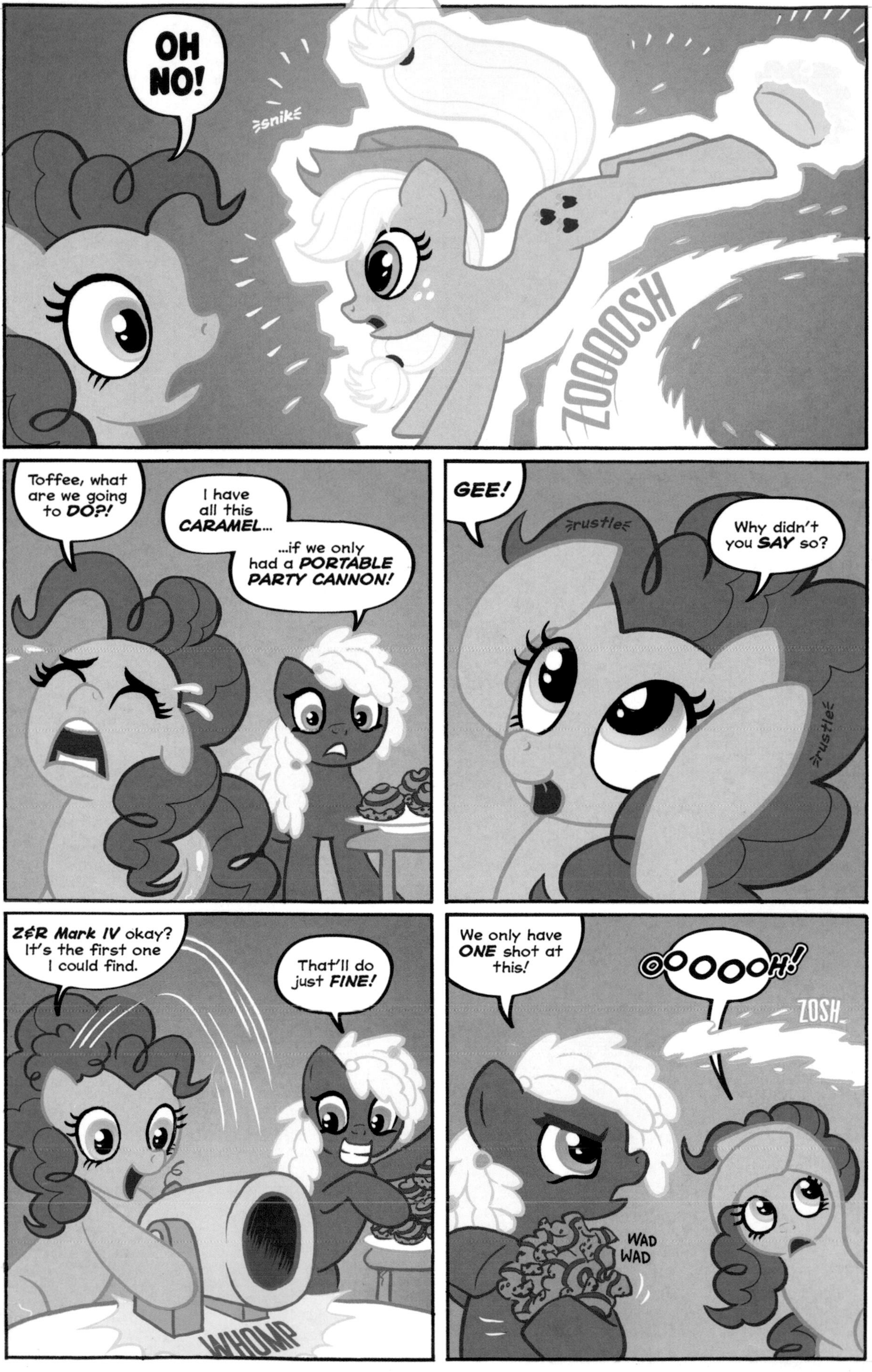

OH NO!
snik
ZOOOOOSH
Toffee, what are we going to DO?!
I have all this CARAMEL...
...if we only had a PORTABLE PARTY CANNON!
GEE!
rustle
Why didn't you SAY so?
rustle
Z&R Mark IV okay? It's the first one I could find.
That'll do just FINE!
WHOMP
We only have ONE shot at this!
OOOOOH!
ZOSH
WAD WAD

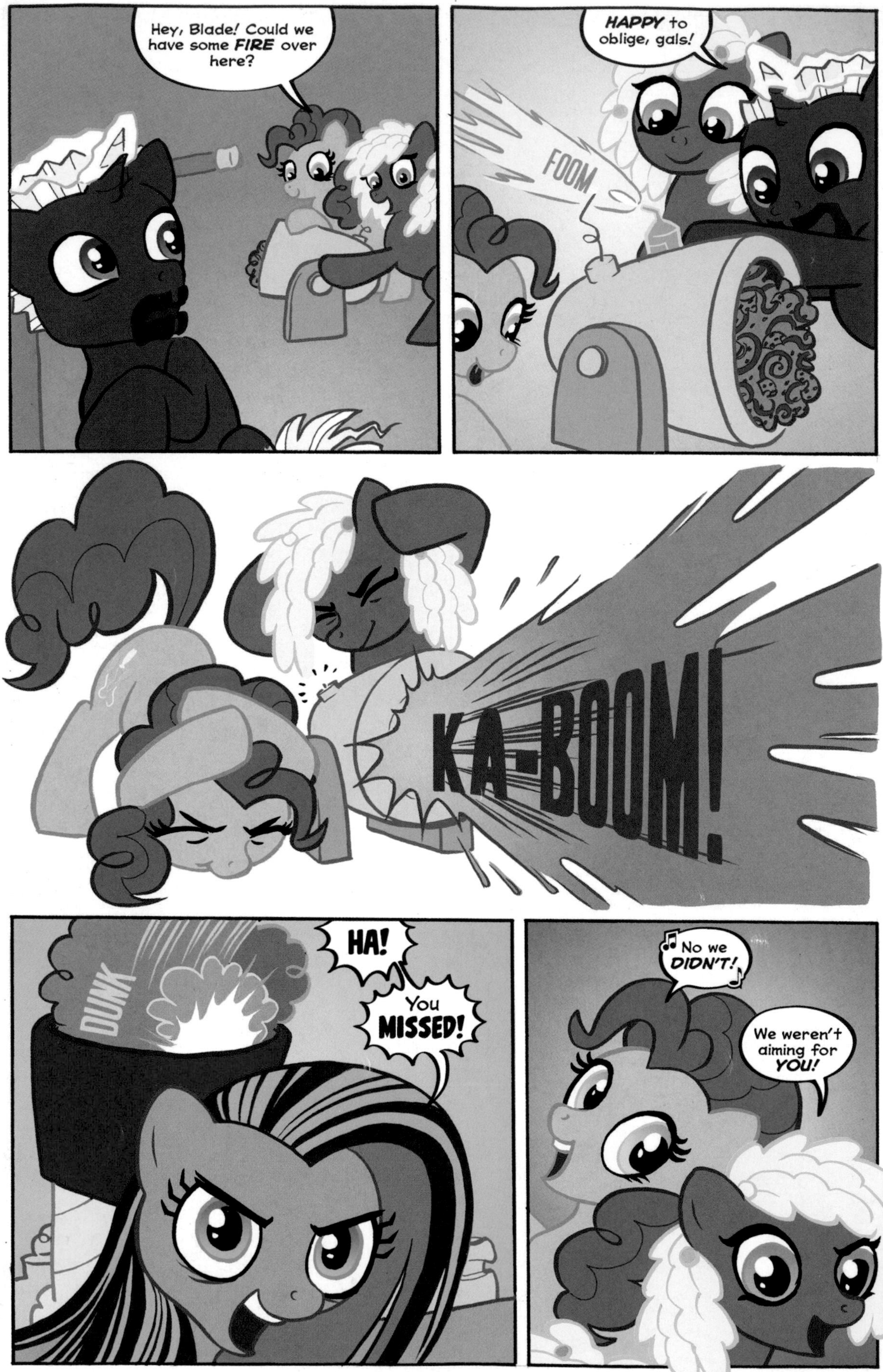

Hey, Blade! Could we have some FIRE over here?
HAPPY to oblige, gals!
FOOM
KA-BOOM!
DUNK
HA!
You MISSED!
No we DIDN'T!
We weren't aiming for YOU!

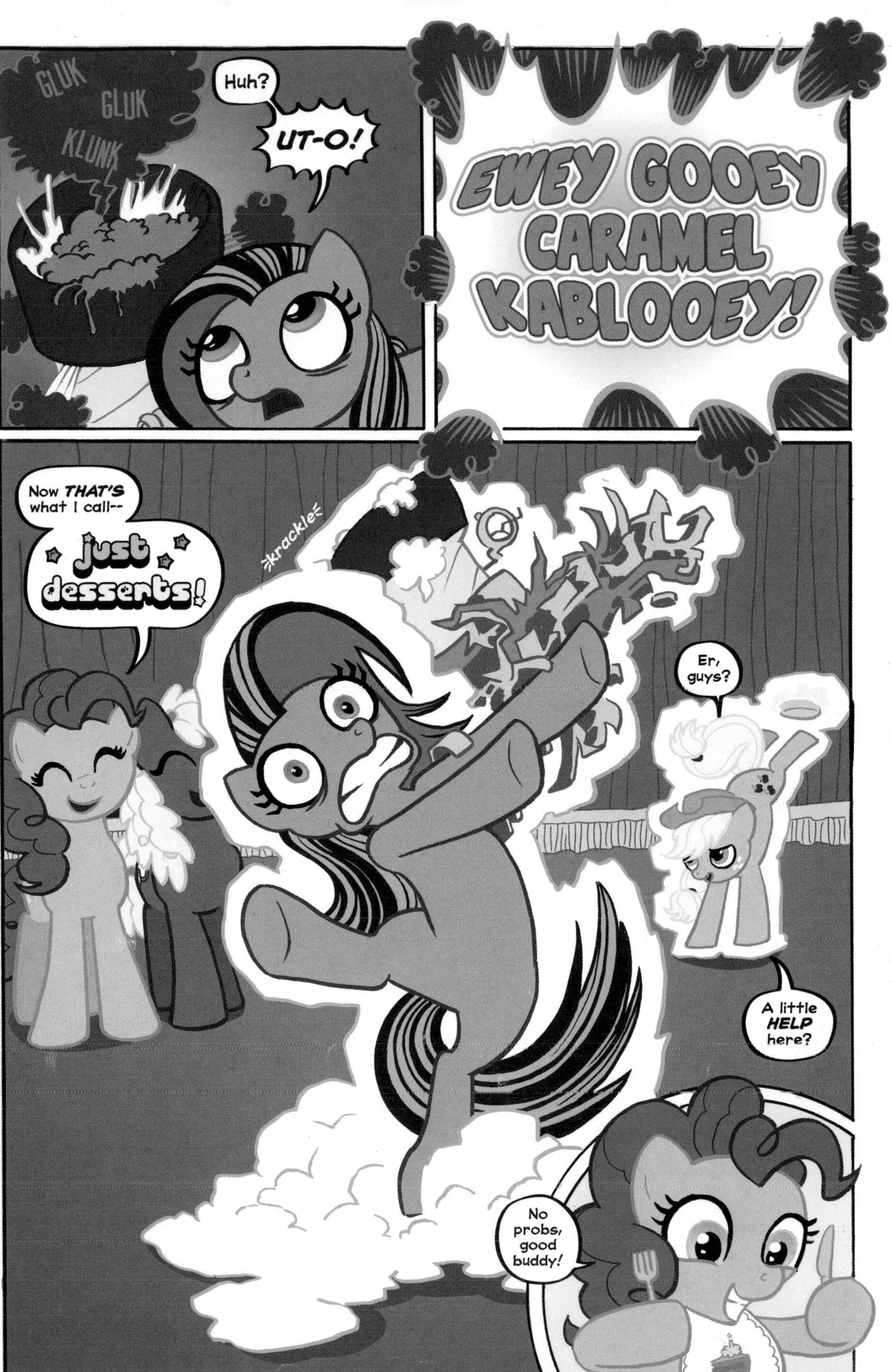

GLUK
GLUK
KLUNK
Huh?
UT-O!
EWEY GOOEY CARAMEL KABLOOEY!
Now THAT'S what I call--
just desserts!
krackle
Er, guys?
A little HELP here?
No probs, good buddy!

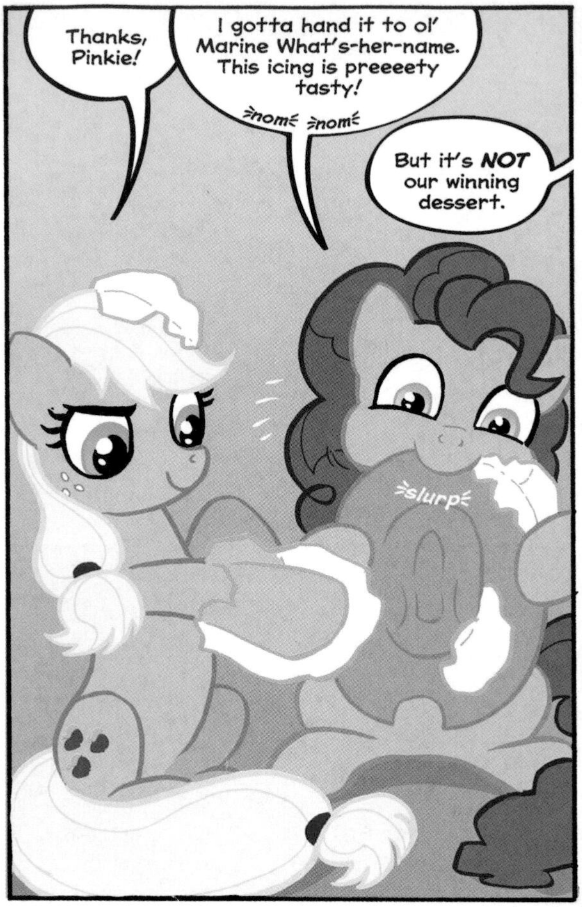
Thanks, Pinkie!
I gotta hand it to ol' Marine What's-her-name. This icing is preeeety tasty!
nom nom
slurp
But it's NOT our winning dessert.

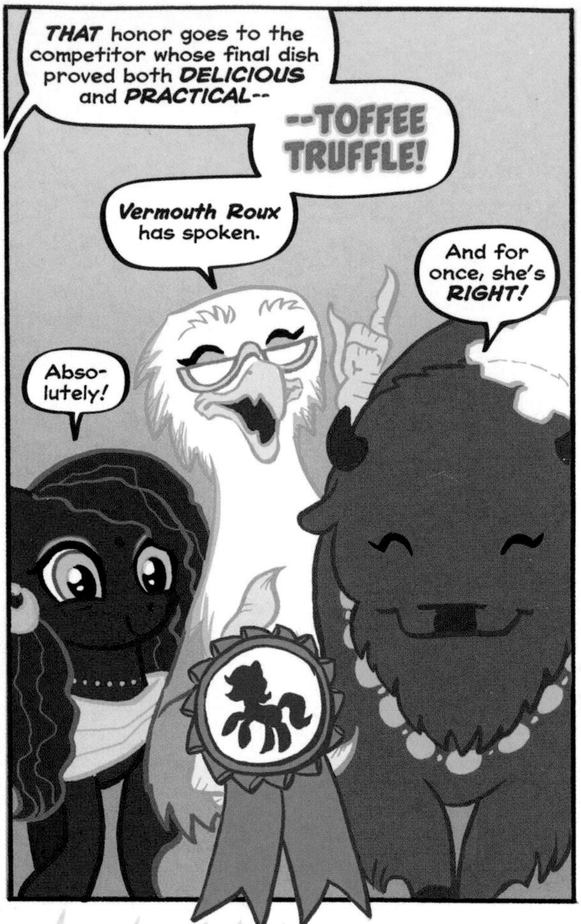
THAT honor goes to the competitor whose final dish proved both DELICIOUS and PRACTICAL--
--TOFFEE TRUFFLE!
Vermouth Roux has spoken.
And for once, she's RIGHT!
Abso-lutely!

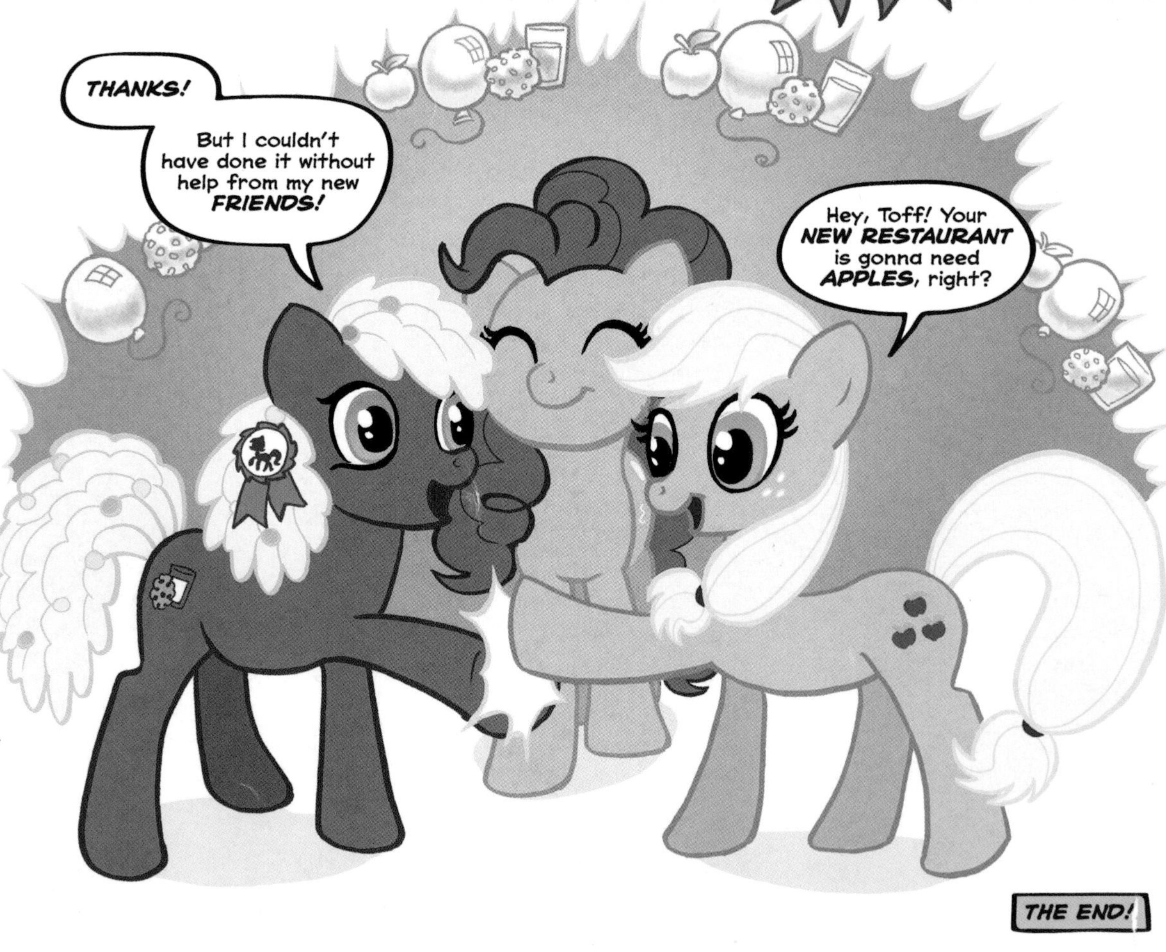
THANKS!
But I couldn't have done it without help from my new FRIENDS!
Hey, Toff! Your NEW RESTAURANT is gonna need APPLES, right?
THE END!